The Picnic
and
Rick Gets It

Written by
Robin Twiddy
& Gemma McMullen

Illustrated by
Amy Li

Can you say this sound and draw it with your finger?

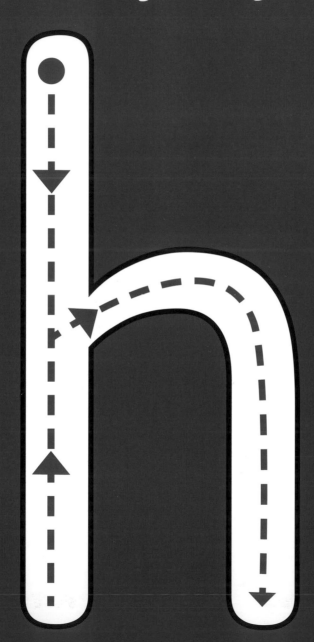

The Picnic

Written by
Gemma McMullen

Illustrated by
Amy Li

Kim has a dog.

Rod has a bag.

A bag and a hat.

Kim's dog gets the hat.

Meg has a bucket.

A bucket and a doll.

The dog gets the doll.

Ben has a rocket.

The dog gets the rocket.

Sam has a picnic.

The dog gets a picnic.

The kids get a picnic.

Can you say this sound and
draw it with your finger?

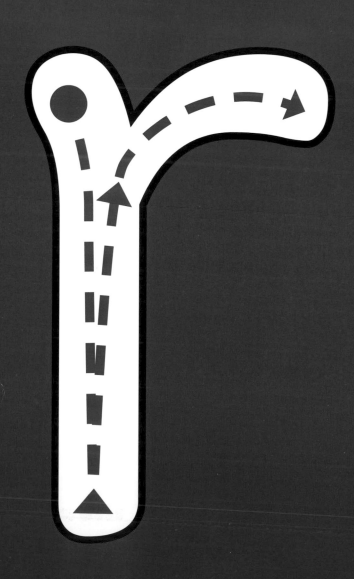

Rick
Gets It

Written by
Robin Twiddy

Illustrated by
Amy Li

Ella has a pet.

It is Rick the dog.

Run, Rick! Go get it.

Rick gets it, but...

... No, Rick!

Run, Rick! Go to get it.

Rick gets it, but...

... No, Rick!

Run, Rick! Go get it.

Rick gets it, but...

... No, Rick!

Run, Rick! Run, Ella!

BookLife
PUBLISHING

©2021 **BookLife Publishing Ltd.**
King's Lynn, Norfolk PE30 4LS

ISBN 978-1-83927-869-3

The Picnic
Written by Gemma McMullen
Illustrated by Amy Li
Rick Gets It
Written by Robin Twiddy
Illustrated by Amy Li

An Introduction to BookLife Readers...

Our Readers have been specifically created in line with the London Institute of Education's approach to book banding and are phonetically decodable and ordered to support each phase of the Letters and Sounds document.

Each book has been created to provide the best possible reading and learning experience. Our aim is to share our love of books with children, providing both emerging readers and prolific page-turners with beautiful books that are guaranteed to provoke interest and learning, regardless of ability.

BOOK BAND GRADED using the Institute of Education's approach to levelling.

PHONETICALLY DECODABLE supporting each phase of Letters and Sounds.

EXERCISES AND QUESTIONS to offer reinforcement and to ascertain comprehension.

BEAUTIFULLY ILLUSTRATED to inspire and provoke engagement, providing a variety of styles for the reader to enjoy whilst reading through the series.

AUTHOR INSIGHT: **ROBIN TWIDDY**

Robin Twiddy possesses a Cambridge-based first class honours degree in psychosocial studies. He also has a certificate in Teaching in the Lifelong Sector, and a post graduate certificate in Consumer Psychology. A father of two, Robin has written over 70 titles for BookLife.

AUTHOR INSIGHT: **GEMMA MCMULLEN**

Gemma is one of BookLife Publishing's most multi-faceted and talented individuals. Born in Newport, Gwent, she studied at the University of Northampton, where she graduated with a BA (Hons) in English and Drama. She then attended the University of Wales where she obtained her PGCE Primary qualification, and has been teaching ever since. Her experience as a teacher enables her to find exactly what makes children focus and learn, and allows her to write books that amuse and fascinate their readers.

PHASE 2
/h/r/

This book focuses on the phonemes /h/ and /r/ and is a red level 2 book band.